Despina Makes a Splash

An Ocean Engineering Story

Written by the Engineering is Elementary Team

Illustrated by Ross Sullivan-Wiley

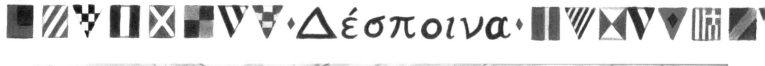

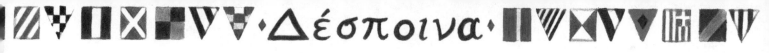

Chapter One | # Something Lost, Something Found

I opened my mouth and sucked in a huge breath. When I felt like my lungs couldn't hold any more air, I ducked my head below the surface of the ocean. I propelled myself forward, carefully holding the boat hook in my hand. Through my goggles I saw a school of skinny sardines swimming by. As soon as I lowered the boat hook a bit closer to them, they flashed and scattered away. I stretched my arm further, trying to snare my cousin Chrisanthy's pink and green goggles. They were hooked over a craggy rock peeking out of the seaweed on the bottom of the ocean floor.

My lungs were burning, but I wanted to reach those goggles! I tried one last time to stretch my arm a bit further. The end of the hook was still too far away—there was no

way I'd be able to reach them. I turned my face toward the sunlight, came back up to the surface, and gasped for air as I bobbed in the water.

"Did you get them?" Chrisanthy asked, calling down from the deck of the boat.

"No," I gulped, still catching my breath. "I saw them but I couldn't grab them. It's way too deep—even with the hook."

"If only your wise older cousin had told you earlier how deep it was here. You would've saved a trip," Nikolas, Chrisanthy's older brother, said.

"So just because you said it's too deep, I shouldn't have even tried?" I asked.

"You're right," Nikolas said. "It's good you tried. I just know this particular spot from experience. I've done research dives here. The water's deep enough so that anything that gets dropped out of the boat sinks out of reach."

"Shoot," Chrisanthy said. "Those were my favorite pair."

"Don't worry, we'll get you some new ones," Nikolas said. "But now I think it's time for Despina to come aboard so we can get back home."

Pulling myself up with my arms, I sat on the sling Nikolas had rigged to hang off the side of the boat. Then

I used the pulley system he created to lift myself up. From there I swung myself down so that I was sitting next to my crutches.

As we started home I watched some of the other boats gliding through the water. I feel like I can glide and swoop and dive when I'm swimming in the ocean, too. When I'm on land, I get around using a wheelchair. When I'm out swimming in the ocean, my arms help me glide and dive through the water. I wouldn't say it's better or easier than when I'm in my wheelchair, because my wheelchair is just like an extension of me. But swimming and being in the ocean is definitely special.

As we sailed back to the dock, the warm wind whipped through my hair. I could taste the salt from the ocean drying on my lips. I watched the coastline of Santorini, the Greek island where I live, until we were close enough that I could pick out my house from the blur of the village. Santorini has lots of hills and stairs, so sometimes it can be challenging for me to move around. When I can't get somewhere with my wheelchair, I have to use my crutches, just like I do when we're on the boat. Luckily, our house is

right on the water, so it's easy to get from there to the dock. As we tied up the boat I could see Mama and Baba working in our yard. When I moved to grab my backpack from under the seat, the sunlight glinting off something floating in the water caught my eye. I inched a bit closer to the stern to get a better look.

"Ready, girls?" Nikolas asked, walking up behind me.

"No, not yet," I said, still peering into the water. I pointed. "Do you see that thing?"

"Yeah," Nikolas said. "Probably a soda can."

"Nikolas, you didn't even look," Chrisanthy said. She squinted and stared at the object I'd pointed to. "It's bigger than a soda can."

"Chrisanthy's right," I said. I turned to Nikolas. "Can you grab the net and fish it out?"

He sighed. "I'm starving and I know your mama has *souvlakia* waiting for us. But for you, anything."

Nikolas grabbed the net off its hook and stretched to capture the object. "Got it!" he called. As he pulled in the net, I turned to get a closer look. It didn't look like anything special. "I think you were right," I said to Nikolas. "It looks like trash."

"I'm not so sure," Nikolas said, carefully removing the object from the net. He flipped it over in his hand a few times. "Actually, I think this could be valuable."

"It's a metal box," Chrisanthy said. "Who would care about that?"

"A lot of people, if it's what I think it is," Nikolas said. "I think it's an instrument used to collect data about the ocean. Despina, I bet this is pretty important to someone."

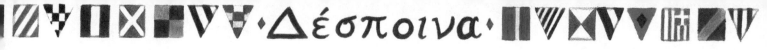

Chapter Two | # An Ocean Treasure?

"A data collection instrument?" I asked, settling myself in my wheelchair on the dock. "Nikolas, how do you know that?"

"Must you always doubt your smart older cousin, Despina?" He grinned and began walking toward home. "It's similar to some of the technologies I learned about in university. All of us studying ocean engineering had to learn about submersibles. That's what we call the vehicles made to explore areas underwater. Ocean engineers design them, and the instruments they carry, to help scientists learn about the ocean."

"But I thought ocean engineers designed ships," Chrisanthy said. That's what Nikolas did for his job—

designed huge ships that moved cargo around the world.

"Some do. But ocean engineers design many different things," Nikolas said. "We all combine our creativity with what we know about math and science to help design things that solve problems related to the ocean."

"What kinds of problems?" I asked.

"Problems like transporting cargo across the ocean, or protecting instruments from the harsh ocean environment," Nikolas said. "Some engineers, like me, design ships. Some design submersibles and the instruments that help people learn about the ocean."

"Like learning about what animals and plants live in the ocean?" I asked.

"Sure, that's one example," Nikolas said. "Ocean engineers might design cameras or recorders on a submersible that capture pictures, video, or sounds from animals. Or they might design instruments that measure the temperature, how salty the water is, or the depth of the ocean floor. That's important for sailors like us to know—we

need to know where the tall rocks and reefs are so we don't hit them with our boats!"

"What do you think this instrument does?" Chrisanthy asked, taking it from Nikolas' hands.

"I'm not sure," Nikolas said.

"I bet it's important!" I said.

"We have to return it," Chrisanthy announced.

"As usual, you're both right," Nikolas said as we reached home and made our way up the ramp to the patio.

I took the instrument from Chrisanthy and turned it around in my hands, looking for a label. "But Nikolas, it doesn't say where it's from."

"Actually, this might be a clue. See this code?" Nikolas asked, pointing to some faint writing on the instrument. "That should help us. Tomorrow at work I'll call a few friends who might know who this belongs to. But now I think it's time for dinner."

....

"Mama! Baba! Wait till you see what we found," I called from the patio.

"I have been waiting," Mama said, shaking her head. "For almost an hour. I was worried you were lost at sea. And now dinner is cold."

I threw my arms around Mama's waist. "I knew you'd be worried. I'm sorry," I said. "But we have a good reason for being late!" I took the instrument from Nikolas and held it out to Mama as a peace offering. "See?"

Mama raised an eyebrow. "That little thing held up your boat, eh? Never mind. Let me look at you. All in one piece?"

"Yes, Mama," I sighed. "We go sailing all the time. Nothing bad has ever happened! Nikolas is an ocean engineer, remember? He designs ships."

"I know, I know," Mama said. "But you can never be too careful."

I sighed again, but knew it was no use to say anything else. I wish I could make her see that I'm all right. That I'll always be all right. I couldn't help thinking, as I'd thought hundreds of times before, that if I weren't in a wheelchair, Mama wouldn't fuss over me quite as much.

Baba joined us on the patio, taking my mind off

Mama's worries. "What's this I hear about you discovering a treasure on today's sail?" Baba asked. "Did you find a statue of a Greek god? An ancient Greek urn?"

"Baba," I laughed. "It's not a treasure. It's an instrument used to gather data about the ocean."

"Really? What kind of data?" Baba asked.

"We don't know yet," I said.

"Nikolas said it could have all kinds of information stored inside," Chrisanthy said. "Data about the water or maybe even pictures of the ocean animals!"

Listening to Chrisanthy, I realized Baba was right. With all the information that could be in that instrument, we might have found a treasure after all. Suddenly I couldn't wait to find out what secrets that little metal box contained.

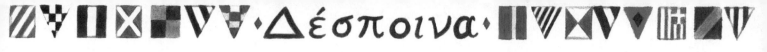

Chapter Three | A Special Trip

A week later I sat on the patio eating breakfast. I kept looking up, hoping to spot Nikolas and Chrisanthy walking down the road to my house. This was the day Nikolas had promised to tell us what he'd found out about the instrument. Every day Chrisanthy and I tried to drag details out of him, but he wouldn't budge. Who did the instrument belong to? What information did it hold? Finally, as I was eating my last spoonful of yogurt, I spotted them.

"Mama," I called, zipping through the house and putting my bowl in the sink. "I'm leaving with Nikolas and Chrisanthy. Be back later."

"Wait, wait," Mama said, coming into the kitchen. "I want to talk to Nikolas before you go. It looks very windy."

I sighed. "Mama, the flag in the yard isn't even

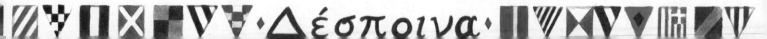

blowing. It's barely windy enough to sail. Remember that time last month when you were sailing with us and it was really windy? Even you admitted the boat was fine."

"At least take a sweater," she said. I forced a smile as she handed one to me. "I packed lunch for the three of you. I'll give the cooler to Nikolas," Mama said.

"That sounds great!" Nikolas called, meeting us in the kitchen. "Lunch from Thia is always welcome on board."

"Hi, Thia," Chrisanthy said. Mama greeted each of them with a hug and kisses on both cheeks.

"Look at you, Nikolas," Mama said. "So skinny, it's as though you never eat."

Nikolas laughed. "No need for you to worry about my eating, Thia. Or about us sailing today. We'll be fine."

"Just watch the weather," Mama said as we began to walk toward the docks. "I heard it could storm this afternoon." We'd barely gotten off the patio when Mama called, "Don't forget—"

"Be careful!" Nikolas, Chrisanthy, and I said in unison.

"We know," I called. "Don't worry. We'll be fine."

As soon as we were out of Mama's earshot, Chrisanthy giggled. "Thia never stops worrying!"

I rolled my eyes. "It's like she thinks I'm helpless."

"She doesn't think you're helpless," Nikolas said. "She

worries about everyone, not just you."

I shrugged my shoulders. "Enough about Mama. Did you find out who the instrument belongs to? I've been wondering all week. Tell us!"

"I'll do better than tell you," Nikolas said. "I'll show you!" Once we got to the harbor, Nikolas walked down the dock, Chrisanthy and me at his heels.

"Where are you taking us?" I asked, as he continued past our sailboat. He turned and grinned, but headed on. Finally he came to a stop in front of a motor boat at least three times as big as our boat.

"Katerina," Nikolas called up to the deck. A young woman appeared and looked over the side. "Meet Despina

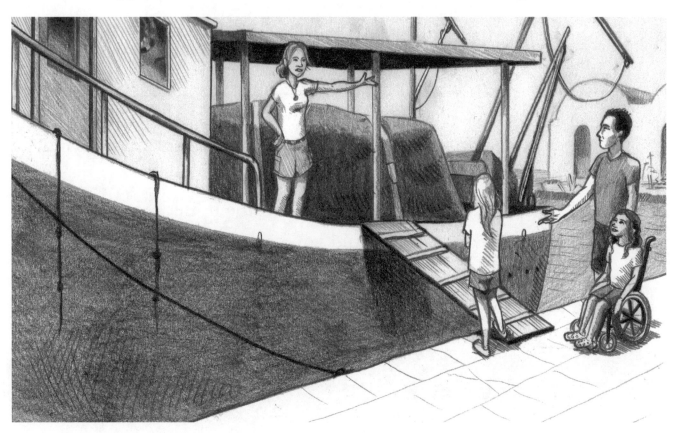

and Chrisanthy," Nikolas continued.

"Our treasure hunters!" Katerina said. She walked down the ramp leading from the boat and stood with us on the dock.

"Katerina is an ocean engineer, too," Nikolas explained. "We went to university together."

"We were so grateful when Nikolas returned the instrument you girls found," she said.

"I'm glad we found it," I said. "Is there important information on it?"

"We hope so," Katerina said. "The scientists haven't had a chance to analyze the data yet. If the instrument worked the way I designed it to, it will have recorded whale sounds."

"Really?" Chrisanthy asked. "What kind of whales?"

"Fin whales," Katerina said.

"We see those all the time when we're sailing," I said.

Katerina nodded. "Some of my coworkers are studying how whales communicate."

"So that instrument can record the noises they make underwater?" I asked. "And you designed it?"

"Yes, but not alone," Katerina said. "I'm part of a team. I work with other engineers and scientists to understand what their equipment needs to do. Then *Thetis* takes those instruments down for a dive."

"Who's *Thetis?*" Chrisanthy asked.

Katerina laughed. "I guess *Thetis* is really more of a 'what' than a 'who.' I'll show you."

I switched from my wheelchair to my crutches so we could follow Katerina on board. She led us to a big cube-shaped frame made from metal pipes. It was just a little bit shorter than Chrisanthy and me. Lots of lights and boxes were strapped to it. Something that looked like a robot's arm reached out from the front. "Here she is: *Thetis.* Our

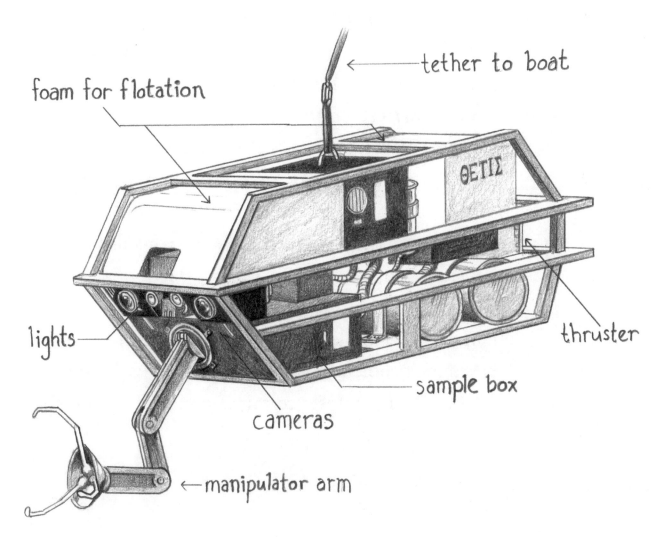

foam for flotation

tether to boat

lights

thruster

sample box

cameras

manipulator arm

Remotely Operated Vehicle—ROV for short," Katerina said.

"I've never pictured a sea goddess like this," Chrisanthy said. I smiled. In Greek mythology, Thetis is one of the many goddesses of the sea.

"*Thetis* really doesn't look much like a sea goddess," I agreed. "But she also doesn't look anything like what I thought a submersible would be. I thought submersibles were like submarines. Or at least something you could ride in."

"I hear that a lot," Katerina said. "No one rides in the ROV. Instead we're able to steer it from here on the boat using remote controls. It's easier for us to work with an open frame like this than something that's enclosed. We can attach different instruments and tools to the frame. And we can easily change *Thetis*'s density."

"Density?" Chrisanthy asked. "What's that?"

"Density is the word we use to talk about how packed something is," Nikolas said. "If there's a lot stuff—or matter—packed into a certain space, we say it's dense, or has a high density."

"I'm not sure I get it," I said.

"Hmm . . . " Nikolas paused for a moment. "I know! It's like the lunch cooler that Thia packed for us." He picked it up. "The cooler contains a certain amount of space—that's its volume. Its volume never changes."

"Right," I agreed.

"But the amount of stuff your mama jams in there definitely changes," he said. "That changes the mass, or the weight of the cooler. After your mama's tomatoes have ripened, she'll load the cooler with tons of juicy tomatoes. The cooler is densely packed. Then after we've eaten a bunch of them, it's loosely packed. The cooler is less densely packed."

"Okay," Chrisanthy said, "I think I understand density. But why does *Thetis*'s density matter?"

"It's important for making her sink or float," Katerina explained. "When we go on missions, the ROVs go deep underwater, but we design them so they will float a bit. The way *Thetis* floats depends on lots of things, including the temperature and the saltiness of the water. So sometimes we need to change *Thetis*'s density—how packed she is—in order to make her float correctly."

"That makes sense," I said, thinking out loud. "You can make *Thetis* sink or float by changing how much stuff—and what stuff—you pack in her frame."

"Right," Nikolas said. "You two caught on fast."

"There's still one part I don't understand," I admitted. "If *Thetis* floats, then how does she explore the bottom of the ocean floor?"

"Good question!" Katerina said. "That's where the thrusters come in. They're small motors that help push the ROV down, up, and sideways in the water. If the thrusters ever lose power, we want Thetis to be able to come up to the surface naturally, which is why we change the density to be sure she floats."

"Just like the instrument we found!" I said. "If it sank we never would have found it."

"Exactly," Katerina said. "Luckily, *Thetis* is tethered to our boat using this cable. So unlike the instrument you found, *Thetis* won't be able to float away. Inside the cable are electrical cords—that's how she sends pictures and messages back to us."

A radio on Katerina's belt crackled. She checked her watch. "Hey girls, we're just about to put *Thetis* in the water to run some tests. Want to come with us and see her in action?"

"That would be great!" I said.

"What's the mission for?" Chrisanthy asked.

"Come with me," Katerina said. "You'll see."

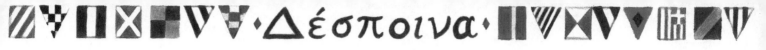

| Chapter Four | # *Thetis's* Mission |

Nikolas, Chrisanthy, and I watched as Katerina's team picked *Thetis* up and gently dropped her over the starboard side of the boat into the water. Just like Katerina had said, *Thetis* bobbed on the surface, floating like an ice cube in a glass. Then we went below deck to the control room. Katerina pushed buttons and turned on *Thetis*'s thrusters to control how *Thetis* moved.

"This screen shows us what *Thetis*'s eyes—the cameras on board—see," Katerina explained, pointing to the computer in front of her. "We can see everything she sees."

"It's just like when I'm snorkeling!" I said. "Except *Thetis* can go a lot deeper and see so much more than I can with my goggles."

"That's right," Nikolas said. "Except *Thetis* can capture images of parts of the ocean that we could never see snorkeling. Even with submersibles like *Thetis*, people haven't explored very much of the ocean."

"Really?" Chrisanthy asked. "But there's so much to see!" A spiky red scorpion fish swam across the screen as if to prove her point.

"It's true," Katerina said. "It's not that people aren't curious, it's that there's so much to explore! Sea creatures and plants on the ocean floor. Rocks and reefs. Oh, good, here's something to show you."

Katerina moved a joystick. "One of the reasons for this

mission is to gather some rocks we wouldn't normally be able to reach."

"Look here," Nikolas said, pointing to the video screen. I saw a robotic arm reach out and lift a large rock from the ocean floor.

"Yay, *Thetis*," Katerina said. She turned to us. "We just designed that new arm for *Thetis*. Today is the first time we're testing it out."

Katerina's mention of *Thetis*'s new arm suddenly made me realize something. "If we were on the other side of the bay, I bet we could pick up Chrisanthy's goggles."

"I wish we could!" Chrisanthy said. "I miss those goggles."

"I think that's a great idea," Nikolas said.

"We can take *Thetis* there?" Chrisanthy's eyes were wide.

"Sorry," Nikolas said. "I don't think that's part of her mission today. What I meant was that I'm sure you could design a technology to help you retrieve the goggles."

"Stop teasing, Nikolas," I said. "We couldn't design something like this."

"Besides, do you think they're even there anymore?" Chrisanthy asked. "The ocean currents could have moved them."

"The currents aren't very strong in the harbor where your goggles were lost," Nikolas said. "What happened to my bold sister and determined cousin? You don't need to design a submersible as complex as *Thetis*. Something simple using some of the ideas we talked about today will probably work."

I could feel my heart beating faster. "Maybe. When you dropped the goggles they were really hooked onto that rock. I bet they're still there."

"Do you think we could do it?" Chrisanthy asked. "Whatever we design would have to be a lot simpler than *Thetis*."

"Some technologies are really simple," Nikolas said. "A technology is just any thing or process designed to help you solve a problem."

"Some ROVs are much less complicated than this one," Katerina said. "*Thetis* is pretty complex because she has many different jobs to do. But some ROVs just do one thing, like record the temperature. It all depends on your goal."

"What do you think?" Chrisanthy asked me.

"Let's do it!" I said. "Mission Goggle Rescue starts today!"

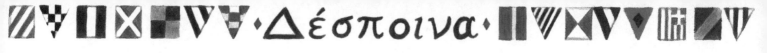

Chapter
Five

Our Own
Design

Chrisanthy and I were so excited, we forgot to stop
and eat the lunch Mama had made. We came home with the
cooler still full—still densely packed! She was really upset.
When we explained our plan, though, she calmed down. She
even said we could fill the kitchen sink with water to quickly
test some materials to see if they would sink or float. And, of
course, she laid out a snack for us on the patio.

After we'd dropped some materials in the sink,
Chrisanthy and I sat on the patio with a bucket of markers
and a stack of paper between us. We were trying to sketch
out ideas for making our own ROV.

"The rock where the goggles are caught is really deep,"
I said, drawing what I'd seen underwater when I first tried

to grab the goggles. "So whatever we design will have to be able to get down to the ocean floor." I circled that spot in red.

"Right," Chrisanthy said, "but we should probably design something that floats, like Katerina explained. The question is how to get it down to the bottom."

"Oh, I know!" I said. "The toy motorboat that Nikolas gave me for my name day celebration! I bet we could use the motor from that in the same way they use the thrusters on *Thetis*."

"That's a great idea," Chrisanthy said. She picked up some paper and a marker and sketched a bit. "What if it looked like this?" she asked. "We need an arm and a hook to grab the goggles, and we need a long rope to tether it to Nikolas's sailboat." She pointed to the parts on her drawing.

"Yeah, that's good," I said. "But what do you think we can make it out of? Whatever we use has to go in the water."

"We can't use paper or materials that get soggy and fall apart," Chrisanthy added.

"Right," I agreed. "And we'll have to think about the density of the materials we use, like Nikolas and Katerina told us. I think some foams and plastics aren't very dense. I'm not sure, though. This might be harder than we thought."

"Hold on," Chrisanthy said, jumping up from the table and running into the house. She came back a few seconds later, dragging Nikolas by the hand. "Come on, Nikolas," she said. "You're an ocean engineer—tell us what to do."

"Chrisanthy!" I said. "We're just getting started! We can do it ourselves."

"But it will be so much easier if Nikolas just tells us," Chrisanthy said.

"I have an idea," Nikolas said. "I know you can come up with a design all on your own. But I do have a tool that I use at work that might help you. It's called the engineering design process."

"Great," Chrisanthy said. "Maybe we can use that. Where is it?"

"Right here," he said, tapping his head. "And here," he continued, tapping Chrisanthy on the head, and then me. "Not all tools are carried in a toolbox. The engineering design process is a way of thinking and working through problems."

"Okay," I said, "how do we get started?"

"You've already started," Nikolas said. "The first step is asking good questions and understanding how others have solved similar problems."

"We did that by asking about *Thetis*!" I said.

"Right," Nikolas said. "And you're doing the second step now, which is imagining ideas."

"We have lots of ideas," I said. "We just don't know what to do next."

"The next step of the engineering design process is to make a plan," Nikolas said. "You can use just one idea you imagined, or combine a bunch of your ideas into one design. Then you need to plan it out carefully."

"But how do we know if our plan will work?" Chrisanthy asked.

"Sometimes you don't know," Nikolas said. "You just have to use what you do know to help you decide."

Mama appeared at that moment to collect our plates. "I'm not sure this is going to work," Chrisanthy said.

"Don't fret so, Chrisanthy," Mama said. "Just give it a try. I've been listening to you girls from in the kitchen. I think your design is going to work."

Did I just hear what Mama had said? "Thia is right," Nikolas said. "When you create your design, which is the next step of the engineering design process, and test it, you'll be able to see if you need to make changes. That's the last step: improving your design. Then you can improve your design again and again until it's the best it can be."

"See?" Mama asked. "I told you not to worry. I'm sure you two will figure it out." With that, Mama went back in the house.

My jaw dropped. I turned to Chrisanthy and Nikolas to see if they'd noticed Mama's new attitude. Nikolas winked as if he, too, were saying, "See? I told you not to worry."

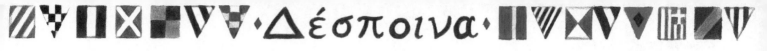

Chapter Six | # Mission Goggle Rescue

It took us a week to come up with a technology we thought would work for grabbing Chrisanthy's goggles. We brought parts of our design to the shallow water on the beach to test if they would float or sink. At first our technology sank to the ocean floor, just like the anchor on Nikolas' boat. But after we made some changes, we were finally ready to bring our design on the boat with Nikolas. Mission Goggle Rescue was ready to go.

I could feel butterflies in my stomach as we sailed to the spot where Chrisanthy's goggles had dropped to the ocean floor.

"Okay, this is the spot," Nikolas said, looking at the GPS screen that confirmed our location. He moved from

the wheel to drop the anchor overboard. "Tell me how your design should work."

Chrisanthy held our submersible. I pointed to the claw we had designed. "This is the part that we'll steer down and hook onto the goggles, we hope," I said. "And this long rope will keep it connected to the boat. One of us just needs to dive in to watch how it's moving. Do you want to do it?" I asked Chrisanthy.

"No way," she said, shaking her head. "You're a much better swimmer than I am. Plus, I don't have my goggles to let me see where it's going!"

I laughed. "That's true. I'll jump in, and I'll point to tell you which way to move it with the controls."

I lifted myself onto the side of the boat and pushed off,

dropping into the salty water.

"Okay," I called. "You can drop the submersible now."
With a splash our submersible hit the water and bobbed next
to me.

I put on my goggles and dipped my face in the water,
searching for the rock and the pink and green goggles.

"I see them!" I said. "Send it down."

I took a breath and lowered my face into the water,
watching the submersible move down toward the ocean
floor. I motioned with one hand to Chrisanthy and pointed
to the right. A few seconds later I looked up. "You're right
over it," I called. "Just move down a little bit more." I
turned my face back to the water. Our submersible slowly
approached the rock, then bounced away without the

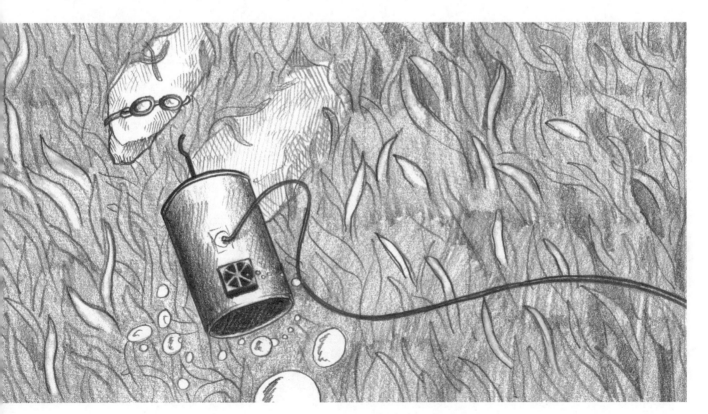

goggles. Darn! I popped up again. "You're right there. Try lifting it up and then lowering it again." The submersible sank again, edging toward the goggles. Closer, closer. I could see the claw touching the strap of the goggles. I signaled them to pull the submersible up. It worked! The goggles were hooked to the claw.

"We did it!" I called.

"I can hardly believe it," Chrisanthy said.

"Here comes your proof," Nikolas added as our submersible floated to the surface and he pulled up the last few feet of the tether. The goggles broke through the surface of the water, dangling from the claw.

Chapter Seven | Celebrating Success

As the boat sailed back home and I looked at the coast of Santorini, a fluttering on the dock caught my eye. As we got closer I could see it was two people waving: Mama and Baba.

Baba grabbed the line I tossed him and wrapped it around the mooring. "What are you doing here?" I asked.

"We had to find out how your recovery mission went," Mama said. Her eyes were sparkling.

"Really?" I asked. "You weren't worried even a bit about the strong wind today?"

"No," Mama said. "I promise. You girls worked hard all week. I thought you did a great job engineering, and I wanted to see how things went."

"It's true," Baba said. "It was all she talked about all afternoon."

"Well, it worked!" Chrisanthy said, holding up her goggles.

"Bravo!" Mama and Baba cheered. "You did it, Despina," Mama said.

"Are you surprised?" I asked.

"Not at all!" Mama said. "I learned long ago to stop being surprised by all that you accomplish. I may worry a lot, but I worry about everyone. You know that. When it comes down to it, I know you'll succeed at anything you put your mind to."

"Thanks, Mama," I said. "That means a lot."

"I have treats at home to celebrate your successful mission," Mama said.

"Let's go!" I said.

"Ouch!" I heard Nikolas say. I looked back and saw him holding his hand, a pained look on his face.

"What's the matter?" I asked.

"I just closed my finger in the hatch," he said. "Yikes. That really hurt."

"Well, Nikolas," I said. "You know what you need to do, don't you?"

"What?" he asked.

"Be careful!" Mama said. "Right, Despina?"
"Exactly!" I said, laughing.

Design a Submersible

Use what you learned from Despina and Chrisanthy to design your own submersible. Your goal is to design a submersible that floats and is able to pick up treasure from the ocean floor.

Materials
☐ Tub or basin of water
☐ Small containers (such as empty medicine bottles or film canisters)
☐ Paper clips
☐ Beads
☐ Sand
☐ Gravel
☐ Rubber bands
☐ Magnets

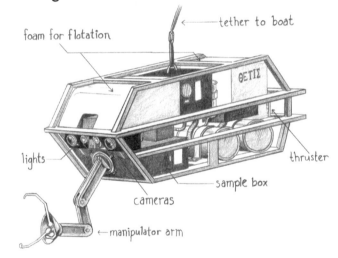

tether to boat
foam for flotation
ΘΕΤΙΣ
lights
thruster
cameras
sample box
← manipulator arm

Ask About Floating and Sinking
Fill the containers as shown in the picture above. Fill one container with sand, one with beads, and one with paper clips. Then fill three more containers so they are half full with each of those materials. Each container represents one instrument that your submersible could carry on its mission. Test each container in the basin of water. Which containers float or sink? Do you notice any patterns?

Prepare packages of "treasure" that you will try to retrieve during your mission by filling three containers with gravel. Use a rubber band to attach a magnet to each container.

Imagine and Plan
The container filled with sand will represent the battery of your submersible. The container filled with paperclips will represent lights. Use a rubber band to attach those containers together. This will be the base for your submersible. Imagine which other instruments you would like to take on your mission, and which combination of instruments you think will allow your submersible to float. Then plan one design by drawing a picture of your submersible. You will need to attach a magnet to your design. The magnet will help you pick up the treasure, just like *Thetis's* mechanical arm did.

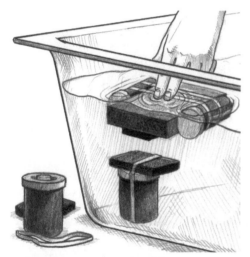

The Goal

Imagine
Plan
Create
Improve
Ask

Create Your Submersible

Build your submersible as shown on the drawing you created. Use rubber bands to attach the instruments. Test your submersible in the basin. Does it float or sink? If it sinks, use what you learned about floating and sinking during the "ask" step of the engineering design process to redesign your submersible so that it floats. Once your submersible floats, use your hand to push it down to one of the packages of treasure. Can it pick up a treasure from the bottom of the basin without sinking? Can it pick up more than one package of treasure at the same time?

Improve Your Submersible

Can you improve your submersible? Use the Internet or go to the library to learn more about different types of submersibles. Can you design a submersible that is able to carry more instruments and pick up more treasure, but still float?

Glossary

Baba: Greek word for Dad. Pronounced *BAH-bah*.

Density: The word used to describe how packed something is. An object's density depends on both its volume and its mass.

Engineer: A person who uses his or her creativity and understanding of mathematics and science to design things that solve problems.

Engineering design process: The steps that engineers use to design something to solve a problem.

GPS: Abbreviation for the term Global Positioning System. GPS is a navigation system that uses satellites to help determine its location.

Name day: The tradition of celebrating a specific day of the year that is associated with a person's name. In Greece, the name day for someone named Despina is November 21st.

Ocean current: The continuous movement of ocean water as a result of forces acting on the water.

Ocean engineer: An engineer concerned with solving problems related to the ocean.

ROV: Abbreviation for the term Remotely Operated Vehicle. An ROV is a type of submersible.

Souvlakia: Greek food made from pieces of meat and vegetables grilled on a skewer. Pronouced *soo-VLA-kee-ah*.

Submersible: A vehicle designed to explore underwater.

Technology: Any thing, system, or process that people create and use to solve a problem.

Thia: Greek word for aunt. Pronounced *THEE-ah*.